This book belongs to

. . . .

For Max and Bella
with love from Richard

For Scot, Corrinne
and Cooper
with love from Lindsey

WE WANT A PET!
A RED FOX BOOK 978 1 862 30908 1

First published by Red Fox, an imprint of Random House Children's Publishers UK
A Random House Group Company This edition published 2013

1 3 5 7 9 10 8 6 4 2

Text copyright © Richard Hamilton, 2013 Illustrations copyright © Lindsey Gardiner, 2013
The right of Richard Hamilton and Lindsey Gardiner to be identified as the author and illustrator of
this work has been asserted in accordance with the Copyright, Designs and Patents Act 1988.
All rights reserved
Red Fox Books are published by Random House Children's Publishers UK,
61–63 Uxbridge Road, London W5 5SA

www.randomhousechildrens.co.uk
www.randomhouse.co.uk

Addresses for companies within The Random House Group Limited can be
found at: www.randomhouse.co.uk/offices.htm
THE RANDOM HOUSE GROUP Limited Reg. No. 954009
A CIP catalogue record for this book is available from the British Library.
Printed in China

We Want a Pet!

Richard Hamilton and
Lindsey Gardiner

RED FOX

We want a pet!

We want a pet!

Please will you let
us have a pet?

NO!

We will not let
you have a pet.
We are dead set
against a pet!

Dogs like to dig,

Dogs like to bark,

Dogs like to walk

in the park.

(And you know what happens on a walk!)

Purrrrr Purrrrrr

Maybe . . .
Could we have a pussy cat?
With soft black fur,
And a purrrrr, purrrrrrrrrr?
We'd like a cat like that.

NO! No cat.

Cats leave hairs
On cushions and chairs.

They scratch

and

snap

And sleep on your lap!

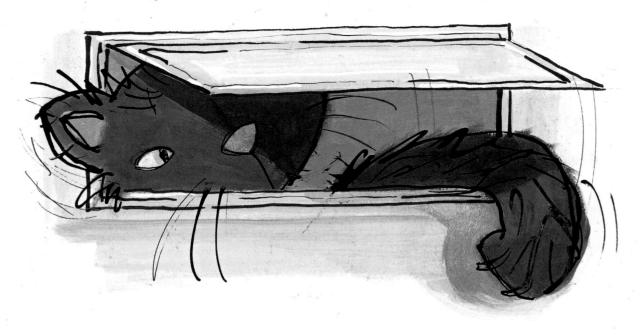

And more than that ~
They need a cat flap!

A rabbit! A rabbit!
We want a rabbit!
A soft and fluffy
bunny rabbit!

No!

Not a rabbit.

Rabbits are sweet,

But they have big feet –

And think how much they like to eat!

Besides, we'd have to clean its hutch.
I tell you, kids, you ask too much:

You cannot have a pet just yet.
We are dead set
against a pet!

Look where we live!
Look at this house!
We don't even have room
to squeeze in a MOUSE!

Forget the pet!
You can't have one!
Now go and play
out in the sun.

So now we lie in the grass,
Watching bugs and beetles pass,
Thinking up a secret plan
To get around our parents' ban . . .

We see legs,

We see eyes,

We see spiders,
slugs and flies . . .

We see bees,

We see fleas,

We see wiggly centipedes' knees . . .

They are small; they're not hairy,
They are quiet, they're not scary!

Wait!

I've had an idea ~
Everything is suddenly clear ~
Our pets are **here!**

Trap the ants,

Catch the snails,

Pick up
the critters

by
the
tail!

Spiders, millipedes,

worms and slugs,

Beetles, caterpillars

and bugs!

Put them in their nice new

homes, and sneak them . . .

Through the kitchen,
through the hall,
To the bedroom
one and all.

Hide them,

Feed them,

Take them out to play,

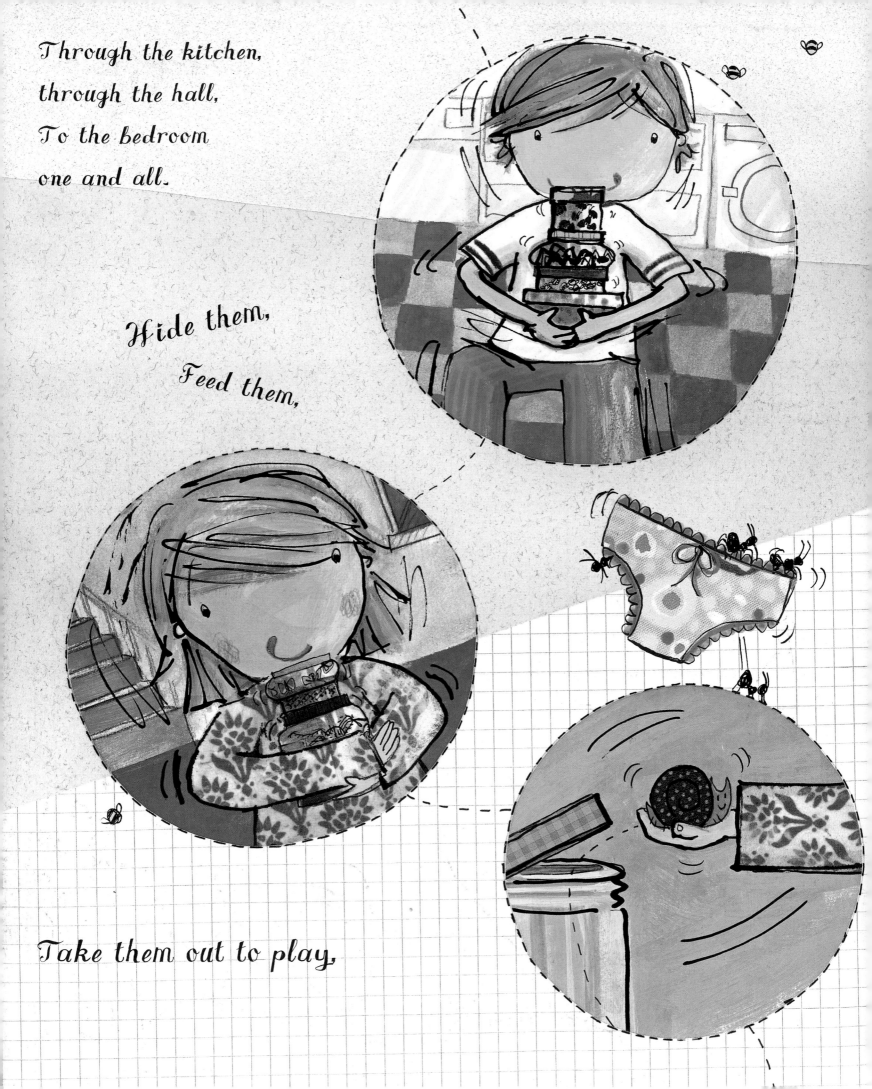

Make them each a collar,

Train them to obey!

Sit, Sally!

This way, Bob!

Until . . .

PUSH!

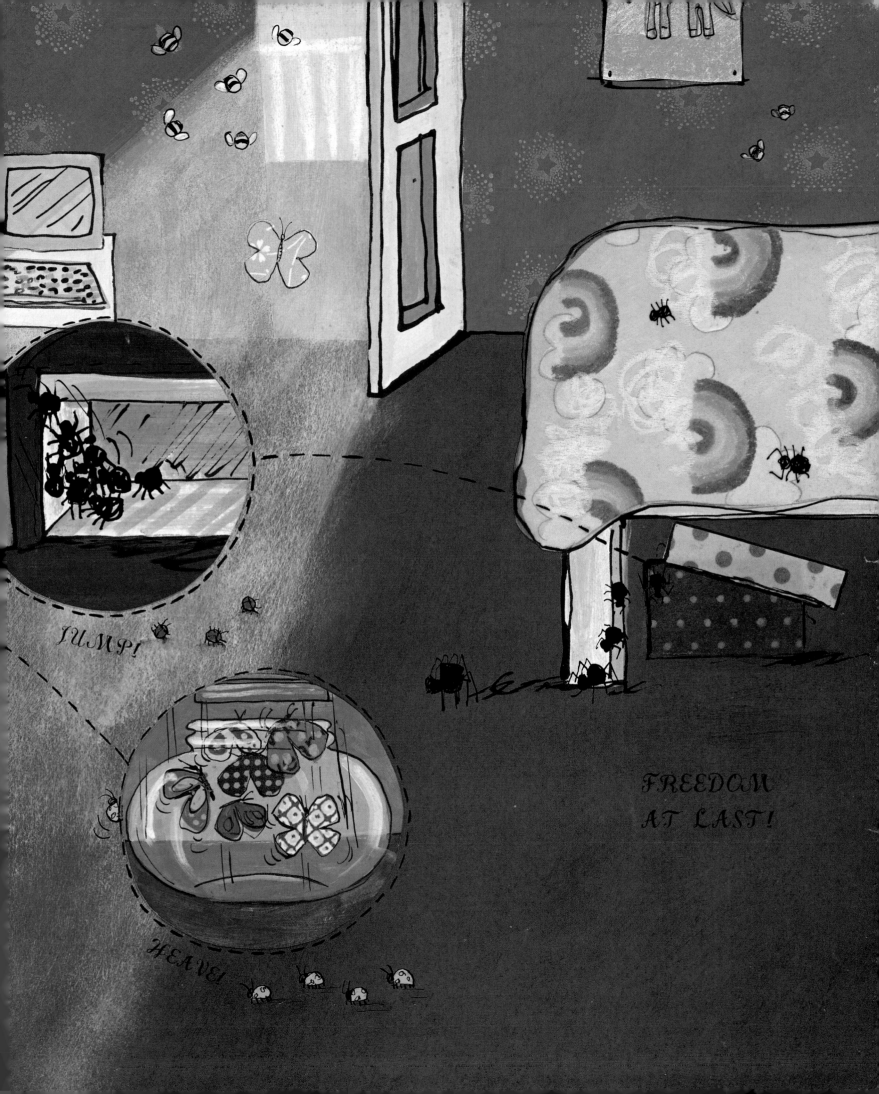

JUMP!

HEAVE!

FREEDOM
AT LAST!

Are those shouts?

Are those cries?

"Eeeek!"

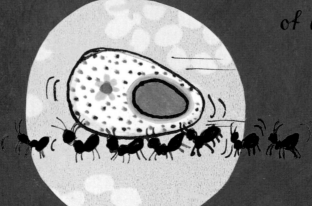

Are those screams
of wild surprise?

"Ugh!"

"Ahhhh! Yuk!"

Children!

What on earth is going on?
Where did these foul things
come from?

These are our pets!

Hector,

Archie,

Sally,

Bob ...

But . . . we said . . .
we could not let you have a pet.

We were dead set against a pet!

Perhaps a little dog instead?